Anna
and the Seven Swans

BY **MAIDA SILVERMAN**

Based on a Baba Yaga tale retold from the Russian by Natasha Frumin

ILLUSTRATED BY **DAVID SMALL**

WILLIAM MORROW AND COMPANY New York 1984

1 2 3 4 5 6 7 8 9 10

Library of Congress Cataloging in Publication Data
Silverman, Maida.   Anna and the seven swans.
"Based on a Baba Yaga tale retold from the Russian by Natasha Frumin." Summary: When her little brother is taken away by the seven swans belonging to the terrible witch, Baba Yaga, Anna searches for him in the great dark forest. 1. Baba Yaga (Legendary character)—Juvenile literature. [1. Baba Yaga (Legendary character) 2. Fairy tales. 3. Folklore—Soviet Union] I. Small, David, 1945–, ill. II. Frumin, Natasha. III. Title.
PZ8.1.S5743An 1984   [398.2] [E]   83-27296
ISBN 0-688-02755-5 / ISBN 0-688-02756-3 (lib. bdg.)

Anna
and the Seven Swans

Once upon a time in a little house at the edge of a great dark forest, there lived a farmer, his wife, their daughter Anna, and their small son Ivan.

One bright summer morning, the farmer said to his wife, "Today is market day in the village. Why don't we go and sell our eggs and fine cheeses?"

"Husband, that is an excellent idea," she replied.

Anna helped her mother wrap the cheeses in fresh green leaves and lay them on wooden trays. The farmer put the eggs into straw-lined baskets. The trays and baskets were put into the wagon, and the husband and wife climbed in, too.

"Anna, my darling daughter," said her mother. "Take very good care of your little brother. Do not leave him alone, or go far from our house. The witch Baba Yaga or her seven swans that steal little children may be nearby."

"Don't worry, Mother," Anna promised. "I'll stay right here and look after Ivan."

The farmer and his wife waved good-bye to the children and drove away to market.

Anna sat Ivan on the soft green grass near the doorstep and gave him a wooden top to play with. Then she decided to make a wreath of wildflowers for her hair.

Anna picked some daisies that grew in the grass
nearby, but it seemed to her that the prettiest flowers
were growing along the path that led into the forest.

Anna wandered down the path, filling her arms with poppies, harebells, buttercups, and celandines. She did not notice that she had strayed far away from her little house.

Suddenly, a great gust of wind came up. It blew the flowers from Anna's arms, whistled loudly in the trees, and shook their branches. Anna looked around, frightened to see that she was almost in the middle of the forest.

"Oh!" she cried. "I forgot that I promised to watch Ivan!" Anna ran back along the path as fast as she could run. But when she reached her house, Ivan was nowhere to be seen.

A sound from the sky made her look up. High above, seven swans were circling, and sitting on the back of one of them was Ivan.

Anna called and cried to the swans, begging them to bring back Ivan. But the swans paid no attention.

They flew higher and higher and finally disappeared behind the dark trees.

Anna ran back into the forest, trying to follow the swans. She knew she must find her little brother and not come home without him. She ran and ran, trying to keep sight of them.

After Anna had been running for a very long time, she came to a big white stove by the side of the path. As she ran by, a voice called out to her.

"Little girl, little girl, why are you running?"

"Oh, Stove," she answered sadly. "I am looking for Ivan, my little brother. Baba Yaga's seven swans have stolen him!"

"Please help me," begged the stove. "My fine cherry dumplings are burning. Won't you stop and take them out?"

Anna was very anxious to find Ivan, but she felt sorry for the stove. So she took the tray of cherry dumplings out of the oven and set it carefully on the ground. Then she ran on.

After a while, Anna came to a gnarled old apple tree growing at the side of the path. As she ran past, she heard a voice calling.

"Little girl, little girl, why are you running?"

"Oh, Apple Tree," Anna replied, "I'm looking for my little brother Ivan. Baba Yaga's swans have stolen him away!"

"Please help me," sighed the tree. "My branches are breaking with the weight of my ripe red apples. Won't you stop and pick them for me?"

Anna wanted very much to run after the swans and find Ivan, but she took pity on the apple tree. She climbed onto its branches, picked the ripe red apples, and heaped them neatly in the grass.

Then she ran on.

After Anna had been running for quite a long time, she came to a river of milk with banks of plum jelly. As she ran past, a voice called to her.

"Little girl, little girl, why are you running?"

"Oh, River of Milk, I'm searching for my little brother. Baba Yaga's seven swans have stolen him!"

"Won't you help me?" asked the river. "I am over-flowing and my jelly banks are melting!"

Anna did not want to stop looking for Ivan, but she felt sorry for the river. She saw three big pitchers in the grass nearby and filled them with milk from the over-flowing river. Then she ran on.

The sun went down, and it began to get cold in the forest. Dark blue shadows on the ground reached up to the dark green tree branches. Anna was too tired to run any farther. She sat down and leaned her back against a tall tree.

"I will never find Ivan now," she thought, and her eyes filled with tears.

Suddenly, Anna heard a great whistling and whirring in the sky above her head. Looking up, she saw seven swans circling above the tree she had been leaning against. Anna looked more closely at the tree and saw that it was not really a tree at all. It was one of a pair of giant chicken legs that were slowly turning round and round. And at the top of the chicken legs was a tiny cottage.

The swans swooped low over the roof, crying, "Baba Yaga, Baba Yaga! Let us in!"

A window was flung open, and the swans disappeared inside.

Anna realized that the swans had taken Ivan into the witch's cottage. She knew she must think of a way to rescue him.

The chicken legs had stopped turning and stood still, so Anna decided to climb up. When she reached the top, she crept quietly to the cottage window and peeped in.

She saw before her a little room. Growing out from each corner and twisting toward the ceiling were the branches of trees, all intertwined. Anna could see many tiny birds fluttering among the twigs, and in the shadow of the biggest branch, an owl with huge, shining black eyes sat watching.

Baba Yaga was sitting in front of the fireplace,
spinning yarn. In a corner near her sat Ivan, playing
with some nuts and apples.

Anna felt very frightened, but she knocked loudly
at the cottage door. Baba Yaga opened it and looked
down at her with a fierce frown.

"Well, little girl," she said. "Why have you come to
Baba Yaga's house?"

"Dear Grandmother,"
Anna replied. "I was
picking flowers in the
forest to make a wreath
for my hair. A wind came
up and blew them all away.
It got dark, and I lost
my way. May I please
come in?"

Baba Yaga rubbed
her hands gleefully.
"Certainly," she answered.
"Sit down by the fire
and spin my yarn for
a while."

The witch gave the yarn to Anna and went outside.
Anna began to spin, and as she spun, she tried to think
of a way to escape with her little brother. Suddenly she
felt something scratching at her shoe. Anna looked
down and saw a large gray mouse looking up at her.

"Little girl, I'm so hungry," he said. "If you will give me some of the porridge cooking by the fire, I will help you and your little brother run away from here."

Anna ran to the fireplace. She spooned porridge into a bowl and gave it to the mouse. He ate it gratefully, and when he was finished, he said:

"Little girl, Baba Yaga is a wicked witch who
gobbles up little children and plays with their bones.
She is outside now, building a fire in her cooking stove.
When the fire is hot, she will cook and eat you. You
must take Ivan and run away, quickly!"

The mouse sat down by the fire. "I will spin the
yarn," he said. "When Baba Yaga calls, I will answer
and pretend to be you."

Anna thanked the mouse.
She picked Ivan up in her arms
and hugged him tight. Then she
ran out of the cottage, quickly
climbed down the chicken leg,
and ran away as fast as her feet
would take her.

After a while,
Baba Yaga called
through the window.
"Well, little girl,
are you spinning
my yarn?"

And the mouse
answered in Anna's
voice, "Yes I am,
Grandmother."

Soon the fire in the
cooking stove was just
right. Baba Yaga went to
the cottage to fetch Anna
and Ivan. She opened the
door and looked around.
The children were nowhere
to be seen. The witch
was furious.

"Swans!" she cried. "My seven swans! Those children have run away! Fly off, find them, and bring them back!" The swans fluttered into the sky behind the cottage and flew away.

Anna, carrying her little brother in her arms, ran along the path through the forest. Soon she came to the river of milk.

"Oh, River!" she cried. "What shall I do? Ivan and I have escaped from Baba Yaga, and she will surely send her seven swans to catch us!"

The river answered, "You helped me when my milk was overflowing. Now I will help you."

The river hid the children under its plum jelly banks. The swans flew by and did not see them. Anna thanked the river and ran on through the forest.

After a while, she came to the old apple tree.

"Apple Tree, Apple Tree, what shall I do?" she cried.
"Baba Yaga has sent her swans to catch Ivan and me!"

"You helped me by picking my ripe red apples when
my branches were breaking," replied the tree. "Now I
will help you." And the apple tree hid the children among
its leaves. The swans flew by and did not see them.
Anna thanked the tree and ran on through the forest.

Soon she came to the big white stove.

"Oh, Stove," she cried. "What shall I do? Baba Yaga has sent her seven swans to catch my little brother and me!"

"You took my fine cherry dumplings out of the oven so they would not burn," said the stove. "Now I will help you."

Anna and Ivan hid under the stove. The swans flew overhead. They circled high in the sky and swooped low over the trees, but they did not see the children.

With a great flapping of wings, Baba Yaga's seven swans circled one last time and flew away, back to the witch's cottage.

"Oh, thank you, Stove," said Anna. She took Ivan into her arms and hurried down the path.

And there, at the edge of the forest, she saw her own dear little house, and her mother and father smiling and waving joyfully to them.